Midge's

Monster Magic

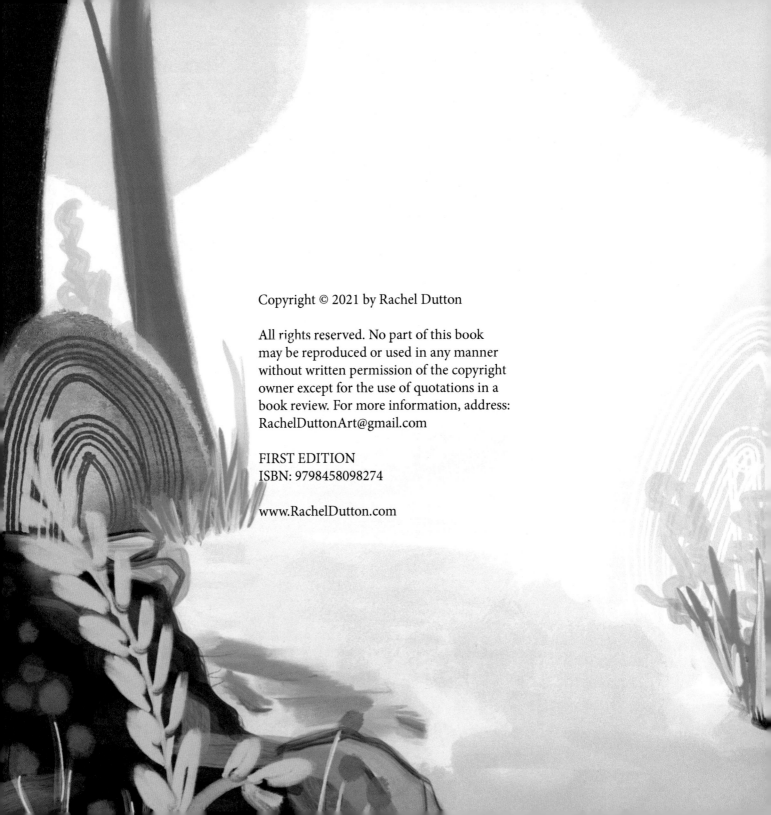

FIRST EDITION
ISBN: 9798458098274

www.RachelDutton.com

Midge was bored.

The whole pond was as dull
as the dirt on a rotten
old log.

"Come play hopscotch!" Hopper hollered.

"Belly-flop contest!" cried Boomboom.

"Tea and flies?" offered Pop.

Midge rolled her eyes.
She had hopped a thousand scotches.

Her belly-flop technique was already flawless.

She didn't even LIKE flies.

She went off alone to wallow.

"MONSTER!"
Midge yelled, but everyone was too busy
playing to hear her.

Midge hopped as high as she could,
but the monster scooped her up
and carried her away.

Her heart flipped and
fluttered like a tadpole!

Would she ever see her friends again?

When the monster finally stopped,
Midge wriggled and jiggled and kicked and

JUMPED!

The monster's face was squishy and warm under
Midge's cold toes. The monster made a MOST
monstrous noise!

Midge landed in a tree
and looked around.

There were monsters everywhere!

They were wrapped in crazy colors, and moved around to wonderful sounds that made Midge feel wild and free and happy.

And they did NOT eat flies.

Midge watched in wonder until all the monsters disappeared, and the night grew quiet and dark.

THIS was the kind of magic the
pond needed!

She got to work.

She couldn't wait to show
those boring old pond frogs
what *real* fun was!

With one mighty leap, Midge soared across the night sky, eager to make her VERY impressive entrance.

But then...

She zigged
and zagged
and zoomed
and snagged!

The other frogs
laughed, but Midge
didn't care.

They would soon
be amazed.

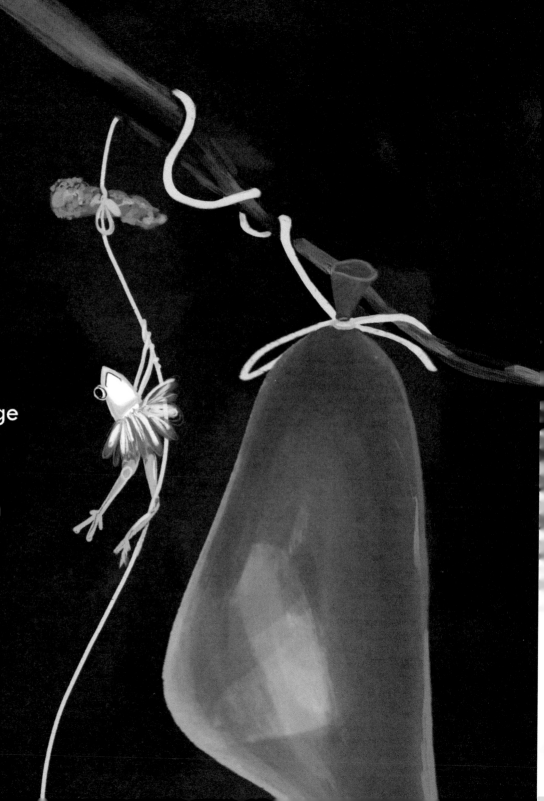

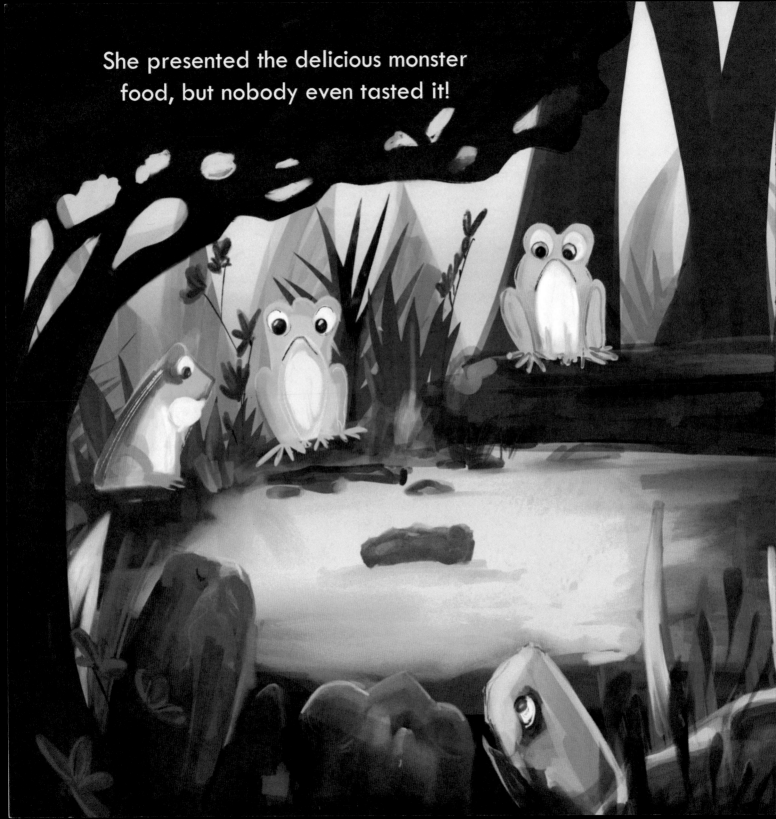

She presented the delicious monster food, but nobody even tasted it!

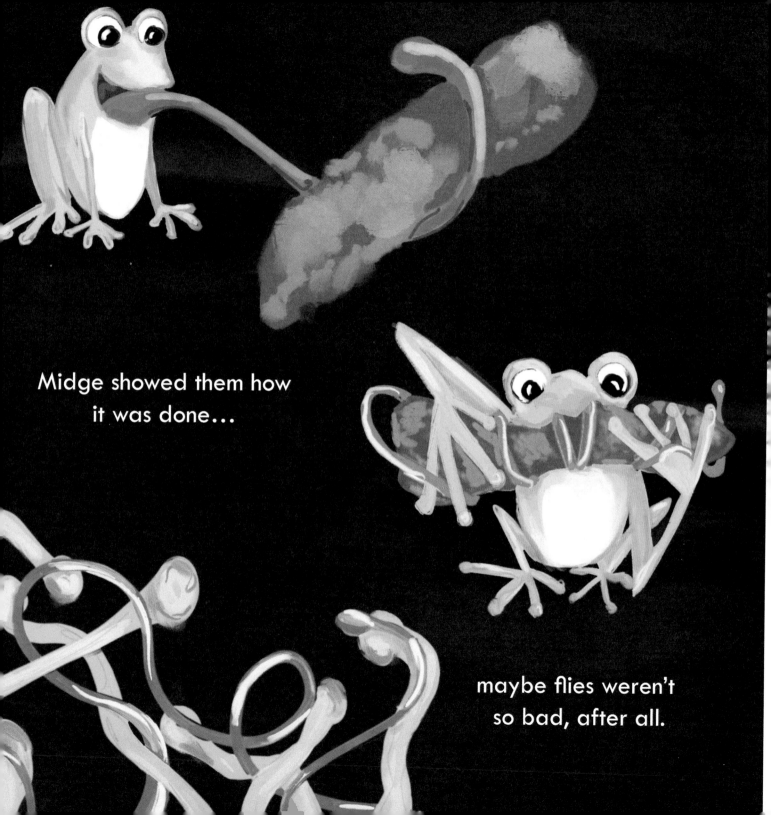

Midge showed them how
it was done...

maybe flies weren't
so bad, after all.

She tried again. Midge donned her bright monster colors and strutted out onto the big branch that hung low over the water. It was hard walking on two feet like the monsters did, but Midge was determined.

Then the wind
started wooshing...

Wooo... ooooo... oooo...

Midge hid under a rock and cried.

None of the monsters' magical things had worked!
She thought she would never make the pond exciting.

"Hey," Hopper said,
"that was some fancy belly floppin'.
Tell us about the monsters!"

"They were amazing,"
Midge said through
her sniffles.

"They made the
happiest music!
They danced wild dances
and sang silly songs."

"We can do that!"
they said.

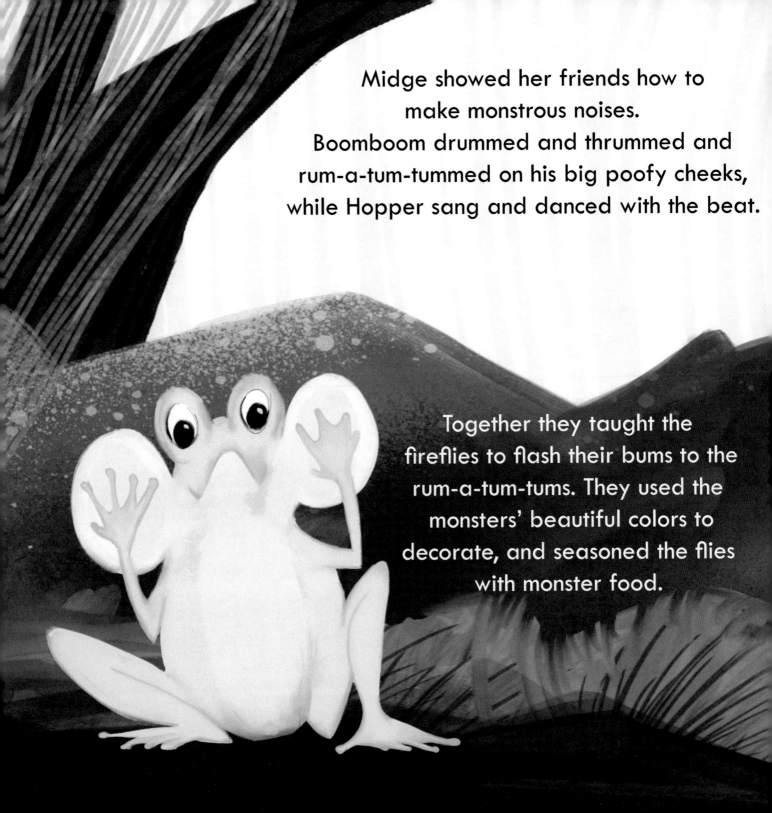

Midge showed her friends how to make monstrous noises.
Boomboom drummed and thrummed and rum-a-tum-tummed on his big poofy cheeks, while Hopper sang and danced with the beat.

Together they taught the fireflies to flash their bums to the rum-a-tum-tums. They used the monsters' beautiful colors to decorate, and seasoned the flies with monster food.

With the crickets singing backup, they put on a wonderful show.
The whole pond booggied and wooggied and hopped and bopped
all night long, and Midge had the best time of all!

She made her own songs, and danced her own dance,
and THAT was the kind of magic the pond needed.

About the Author

Rachel Dutton is a writer and artist. She lives in Arkansas with her husband and dogs, in the woods where there are lots of frogs having lots of parties (frogs love to party).

She is the author of "The Moose Who Loved Noodles," and is working on more silly picture books.

You can get early access to free e-books as well as free coloring book pages at RachelDutton.com

If you enjoyed this book, please help others find
it by leaving a review on Amazon or Goodreads!
Thanks for reading!

Made in the USA
Coppell, TX
06 May 2022

77459447R00021